Ballad of a dead s

CW01666294

life inself feels like there are puppets
in my head
that always feels like death
the master puppets are winning
like damn im to strong getting on
my head recovery still began
yesterday no way in hell im letting
the darkness coming inside me
for the past 2 days have been a deep
challenge for me still not in my closet
damn not I am getting the lonely
coffin in the sky this morning was a
great day woke up is in peaceful

I saw death

My hole like life is like death
Coming back to life many times
Death was like apart of my recovery
For me
Till one death I died saw hell and
heaven at the same time
Some people like darkness
Few like light
When I saw heaven the feeling was
awesome
I now know the path I choose
Many times people tried to kill me
Having faith in god later I am
accepting jesus Christ as my savior

In the battle of spirituality.

Recovering from Russian roulette

Contantly armed in my heart
This game was introduced in a
recovery sister.
At first the game seemed bitter
Sweetness of a blissful misery
Recovering had played this for a long
time.
Had god behind my back
Even when I was homeless I never said
I quit and say die
Deep down never had doubt
Today I have a house to my own

Recovering from everything feel proud
Love the fact I am getting my family back
In this game still got to stay tall
If not all will fall down.
I love my town promised land I still it see it mean hope
I have no hate In my life
Together one day I hope I will be fully recovered from Russian roulette
Till then it's a battle that will end soon.

The talk of the town

Thall shall not kill

Thall shall not kill

Im still the talk of town
Trying to bring me
The best thing is still earn respect
What next for me
Don't they know im trying to have
recovery

Thall shall not kill

Speaking the trueth
Just for one day of peace

Thall not fall
I will aways stay tall

Will never fall or say give up.

Moving on

Moving on from the past
With the voices in my head seemed
not to last
Moving on like a guided spirit
Im moving on.
Very strong headed I will know I will
move on. And everything will be ok

Feeling good for the first time team work

Imagination goes along way
Today I am having a good time
Talking to my mother every day
Means the world to me
Helps in many ways even in many
ways this crazy game og Russian
roulette

The 4th lady
Dedicated to you

I wanted to say thank you to the
Lady who really help me see my

recovery a little bit better
This is for you I owe you a debt to you
4th lady no women today was really
nice

So far seems over

So far it seems over
No wants to believe me
In this Russian roulette
Game in my head it wants me
Dead or my family separated
Supposedly
Been listen to a lot of church music
My church elevation

Progress not perfection
Not every day is a good day but hey
Still alive.

Living in pain,like not

The pain used to be joy
For me really be the judgment
In me not really knowing
The harm I was causing others
Around me
Took me being homeless to be finally
Free of my anger I was a man full
Of danger to anyone around me
Now I taking care of my self I finally
Feel free.

Sometimes

Sometimes I want to be like damn I
Want to give up and cry why is this
happening to me finding out in my
journey this isn't I am not alone
Now I am trapped between 2
decisions to be angry or free today
humbly I choose free forgive all my
enemies I cant stop feeling good I like
this to much I really like this energy
that comes out of me. People say I
should have enough. But I had a lot of
anger didn't quit look where it led me.
Almost dead, definitely homeless on

the street I proved a lot of people
wrong me and my god are too strong
we are like an empty box full surprises
Im here to stay its totally
awesomeness

I gave you my heart and soul

I broke a rule that I would date you
I was fool I feel in love with you
To break up with you I was to scared
When we finally did I was in a lot of
pain that was not need. People were
not pleased I kept talking about pain.
They tried really hard to make me
sane again but I kept going back to

the problem robbing them of there freedom and there peace. I was dead wrong I still have a lot you guys may all you guys rest in peace I home you know my intentions where pure.

I believe

I believe more then ever I can go the distance there be hind me is the past it could stay there with the depression all the misery today I am a winner champion in my own mind its about damn time. Finally in my mind tha past is dead and gone.

he told me I was good for nothing barely passing school always

a lie

seen not cool a total loser feeling
empty I never gave up rose up like a
flower a pedal dead till gone finally
feels like I won no longer a lie just
living life

sunshine

I was addicted to you with an
invitation to your love
For the first time I felt spirituality
My true revelation
I mention this due to love can be an
addiction

Now she wants to call it quits calling me a bum a rummy I let her check out now she is married to a new man Me I am back just to my only thing I cared about is my rum it brightness up my day

Don't break me down

Of you and and I struggled to survive! Call it love, crazy to me you were everything still today, even now you are dead and gone. I realize I wasn't the perfect man, my heart was in right place! Sorry for making your life so hard. Sometimes I wonder if we were still together. Would we love each other? Those questions, I cant answer times past I still have your love! Its like a shadow over me! Constantly, going over me its beautiful pain. I just wish you seen me today more sane. But we always fell back to old ways. I apologize now I cant damn!

Being healthy

Being healthy means everything to me, being a basket case now an ace Graduated from my past now having a blast from getting a lot of people angry at me! One person once said real love lets people go! I still have a hard time dealing with that. Progress! I feel like a plane and sore away. Just to be free from animosity.

Ghetto walls

Not talking knower ghetto's. just the original ones back in world war 2,my god. At that time there was so much hate, one man dictated the fate of the world was being decided by Germany. Luckily Germany didn't take over the world.

But nower days there is a new ghetto.

Where poor people live with people stepping all over them, on the streets, I'm guilty of this I was homeless as well it was hell. I should have died many of times but I didn't I survived. Today I am blessed.

This poem is dedicated to my poppy who fought and survived in world war 2. He was my best friend as a kid.

If

From being an addict an actor then director fighter in my own sick demented show struggling with my own recovery with booze drugs and on top of that mental illness. My life was a complete mess. No time to rest waiting for the next fix. Felt like I was stuck under water drowning. Till one day I finally over did it. Wound up in a hospital. If only they knew my misery maybe they would understand me. But that is quite the paradox, which alone tells a story in its self. I just wanted to shelf my head for awhile and just rest. Finally accepting help I feel free not fearing anyone coming after me anymore. Totally safe!

little do you know

I care about you I screaming to the stars that are far away I know the pain of that all to well feel like hell it makes me wake wake up in a hospital thank god I get another chance at life I cared to much about you that it brought me to my knees beginning me for forgiveness with my god finally realizing I need help one minor yelp to my recovery there are other ways to show people you care and not to go to the extreme thank you for still being a team and not being shady and not leaving me and believing in me I am brand new me hey today is brand new day

outlaw the drama

outlaw the drama develops bad karma destroys families turns friends into enemies drama seems like a no way out sticky situation today I set aside any problem I have turn it all over to god even when things are odd what may seem at the time big and tall are really quite small so outlaw the drama develops bad karma only way to beet it is recovery and serenity

Everything's on fire

Just another beautiful day in this window pain game gotta game of Russian rullet in my head that constantly wants my dead I just recently heard gods quiet during a test but damn seriously when will this game end for me happens to me constantly not every day is a bad day but I can feel the burn from it I just want it to go away its just another kind of window pain when life is already but im like really when is this game going to be over peaks and valleys definitely describes me when I get this way luckily I don't think about a drink or a drug im not feeling sorry for myself in any way or form I keep my faith im like bullet proof with them I keep my faith in god strong

I know how it feels

To be messed up on a daily routine
Of gambling drugs and alcohol being free now from everything now ten years now I can tell you its been a great journey even if I was to be homeless again I would do it again every day I step outside in the cold

To remember how cold it was for me on the streets ripping out important pages from my pages starting fires with them to keep me warm putting paper in my shoes to keep me warm but I did it one year later thanks to my family I have a place to my own we call it my safe place that's exactly what it is I no longer drink drug gamble 10 years now how one day at a time

Living like a poor richess
Dedicated to the two cops who helped me

Living like a poor richess
Went from homeless to homeless
Never gave up or say die

Nor did I shed a tear or cry
Kept my faith in god
His mercy kept me alive
There where two cops that saved my
life. I was going to break
Into a car. Not right I know but these
Cops had a heart. I told them I was
homeless was hungry the cop lady
Gave me food. And the one cop
ubered a taxi for me, its crazy how
you see peoples point of views of
things the took me to the hospital
that cost them well over 200 dollars
And the helped me on my journey
from then on I started my glimpse to

serenity. So thank you to the two unknown cop that helped me

All that

Thinking we all that
Dualities of life
Coming together as one
Waking up at the morning crack of dawn
Smile and put a face on
Another day above ground is like pre heaven
A score before you sore to the heavens

So what I leave you is a bliss full of misery that remain in the past it will remain forever at last

Don't break me down

Of you and and I struggled to survive! Call it love, crazy to me you were everything still today, even now you are dead and gone. I realize I wasn't the perfect man, my heart was in right place! Sorry for making your life so hard. Sometimes I wonder if we were still together. Would we love each other? Those questions, I cant answer times past I still have your

love! Its like a shadow over me!
Constantly, going over me its beautiful
pain. I just wish you seen me today
more sane. But we always fell back to
old ways. I apologize now I cant
damn!

Sometimes

Sometimes I want to be like damn I
Want to give up and cry why is this
happening to me finding out in my
journey this isn't I am not alone
Now I am trapped between 2
decisions to be angry or free today
humbly I choose free forgive all my

enemies I cant stop feeling good I like
this to much I really like this energy
that comes out of me. People say I
should have enough. But I had a lot of
anger didn't quit look where it led me.
Almost dead, definitely homeless on
the street I proved a lot of people
wrong me and my god are too strong
we are like an empty box full surprises
Im here to stay its totally
awesomeness

The pain

The pain used to be joy
For me really be the judgment

In me not really knowing
The harm I was causing others
Around me
Took me being homeless to be finally
Free of my anger I was a man full
Of danger to anyone around me
Now I taking care of my self I finally
Feel free

<u>Seeing things differently</u>

To many tragedies in a short life
When I would be hurting I dreaming
about a better day
Things never went my way
Today finally seem to go that way

Everything dies for something better

Everything dies yet a stone to a rose a whimper a dead loved one
Wondering what if they were to come back
So heavenly you prayed for a day to see them again Everything dies but in a sense Everything rises

I love

I love the way you brought me up in life it was I who destroyed my own life now I'm living average I am telling

you how much I love you words are
not a whimper nor a tear but a
simple joy that I enjoy everyday day
with you
Just remember how things were
between us bitterness not sweet total
not alot fun
May you always rest in peace

<u>Cartoons</u>

You blame me for this new type of
poetry you next my mind is going
crazy seeing a new field of
opportunities books are almost done
for within my poetry I attempt bring

it back with something new
I got nothing to loose
Is a dieing trade rushing in a
cemetery do be afraid expect me I'm
coming

Printed in Dunstable, United Kingdom

67965495R00020